## American Horse Tales

# Camp Mah Tovu

by Yael Mermelstein

Penguin Workshop

Dedicated to Jessica Vitalis,
with gobs of gratitude—YM

**PENGUIN WORKSHOP**
An imprint of Penguin Random House LLC, New York

First published in the United States of America by Penguin Workshop,
an imprint of Penguin Random House LLC, New York, 2021

Copyright © 2021 by Penguin Random House LLC

Visit us online at penguinrandomhouse.com.

Library of Congress Control Number: 2021018938

Printed in the United States of America

ISBN 9780593225332                    10 9 8 7 6 5 4 3 2 1 COMR

# Chapter 1
## Welcome to Camp

Some kids said Camp Mah Tovu was haunted by the ghosts of wild horses that used to live there. But I wasn't afraid of horses, supernatural or otherwise. Actually, riding a ghost horse sounded fun.

"Ouch," I said as I smacked myself in the face with my sleeping bag, which I'd unrolled in the wrong direction. I tend to do things backward.

"I heard there are *real* wild horses here, but they only come out at night," said my new bunkmate,

Becky, plopping her sleeping bag on the bed in the corner, the one I'd wanted to claim. I knew her name because our counselor, Shimona, was making us wear dumb clown name tags.

"I heard the horses have horse bodies and lion heads," said Esmé, a girl as tall as a tree and as thin as a sheet of paper made from that tree. She was dressed in brand names from head to toe, the kind of outfit Mom and Dad would have said "cost an arm and a leg," an expression I always found gross.

Esmé looked at a girl named Sarah like she wanted to get her opinion. According to the bunk list I'd gotten a month ago, they were the only two North Carolina locals attending Mah Tovu. Everyone else came from the New York tri-state area. Sarah looked away, stuffing her pillow into a pillowcase decorated with purple unicorns.

"Yeah," she finally said.

Esmé turned her attention to me. "What do you think, uh . . . Lila?"

"Lion heads would be too heavy for horse bodies to hold up," I said as I claimed the last and worst bed, right in the middle of the bunk. If I snored or drooled, everyone would see. "They'd be bobblehead horses!" The thought made me laugh. And I snort when I laugh. Just add that to the snoring and drooling. Lila Grossberg: Queen of gross bodily things!

My mouth raced ahead of my brain.

"I'm an expert horse rider," I said. "By the way."

That was a fat, wriggling lie. By the way.

"You mean equestrian?" Esmé said, looking skeptical.

"Yup," I said. "That. So, here's hoping we find real live horses. With regular-size heads."

Esmé and Sarah exchanged glances. I tried covering my name tag with my right hand so maybe they'd soon forget who I was. But I was only covering the last two letters in my name, so you could still see the Li—reminding me of what I was, a liar.

I stuffed my canteen money under my bed, between my lucky stuffed toucan and my lucky water bottle. Mom had told me not to pack the "kitchen sink," but I figured I could use every bit of luck this summer.

"Girls, how's the unpacking going?" Shimona said, entering the room with a bright smile.

"They're talking about the horses," a girl named Jilly said. She had straight brown hair scooped into a ponytail reaching past her waist.

Shimona shook her head, sending her blond curls bobbing.

"There's no such thing as a camp without a legend," she said. "I spent the last five years at Camp Shalom, and they were convinced that there was a real bigfoot lumbering around. Some of the counselors got us good when they made huge footprints in the mud after a rainstorm, using an old tire. Trust me, the biggest feet in that camp belonged to Jakey Strauss, and he only wore a size-thirteen shoe."

"So, uh, you don't think we need to worry about them?" Jilly asked, gnawing on her pinkie.

"Not the ittiest bit," Shimona said. "Now finish unpacking, because we're having our first girls' campus kibbutz in an hour."

My heart did a backward flip. Kibbutz was no big deal—just a gathering where the head counselors tried to get us into the camp spirit. But it reminded me of last summer at Camp Reyut. Not that anything bad had happened *specifically* on that day. But it had been the beginning of a *bad* summer. Mom said bad days were like peanuts—they didn't taste especially good, but they were small, and before you knew it, they were finished. But Camp Reyut had been like eating a bag of peanut shells. That's why I'd traveled all the way from New Jersey to North Carolina this year. The farther away from Camp Reyut, the better. This summer would be better. I'd only been nine years old last summer. I was *much* more mature now.

"What time is the kibbutz?" I asked as I chewed on a Shugabird, my favorite treat. They were sugar-covered jelly birds, and my mother had sent me with a monthlong stash. It would probably last me three days.

"No worries, I'll get you guys," Shimona said.

"But, uh, what if you get distracted and forget to call us?" I asked.

"Chill like a cucumber," said Esmé.

When I get nervous, I do the opposite of that.

"Why cucumber?" I asked. "Why not carrot? Or cabbage. Chill like a cabbage."

Shimona's smile faded.

"Or what about fruit, huh?" I asked. "They also live in the refrigerator. Chill like a peach. Or a container of milk, for that matter. But not curdled milk. Ew."

Esmé jabbed Sarah's shoulder with her own. "And she thought lion-headed horses were weird," she whispered, loud enough that I could hear.

I needed to stop talking, but my brain is like a can of soda, and when it gets shaken up, words fizz over without stopping. Before school each morning, I take one tiny pill that keeps my brain from somersaulting all day. But it also makes me feel like a zombie propped on a hanger. This summer, Dr. Donut (that's really his name) decided I didn't have to take my pills to sleepaway camp, and now my brain was doing fully trained cartwheels.

"Or chill like a polar bear," I blurted.

7

"Good one," Sarah said. "Because they live in Antarctica, where it's freezing, right?"

I appreciated her sticking up for me.

I twisted my lips so no sound would come out but—whoa! Out popped more.

"Polar bears don't live in Antarctica," I said. "They live in the Arctic, on the opposite side of the planet."

Everyone was staring at me. Nobody looked friendly. Not even Shimona.

I bent down and tucked my hand under my bed, finding my lucky toucan.

"Some luck you're bringing me," I whispered as I squeezed her beak a little too hard.

Mom was right. I shouldn't have bothered bringing along all this stuff. It wasn't going to help. This summer was going to be a repeat of last summer—another bag of shells for the trash.

# Chapter 2
## Lila Grossberg Is a Fake

Both of our bunkhouse mirrors had a line three girls deep as the loudspeaker blared pre-Shabbat music.

"I love your skirt!" Becky said to Esmé as she spun, her green skirt rising and twirling.

"Thanks. My dad bought it for me."

I love my dad as much as a beaver likes to munch on wood, but he's an accountant who keeps track of numbers all day. I imagined if he'd walk into a girls' clothing store, you'd most likely find him asleep under one of the racks a few hours later.

I stepped in front of the mirror. Mom had bought me a dress with giant sunflower print. We'd both loved it in the store, but now I noticed all the other girls wore skirts and tops.

I brushed my brown hair into a half pony, securing it with a bright yellow scrunchie.

"Let's go, guys," Shimona called as the music stopped, signaling that Shabbat was beginning. "Prayers are at the lake. Bring your siddurim."

Esmé grabbed Sarah's hand, Becky grabbed Jilly's, and Ariella and Marley exited the bunkhouse together. I looked at Shimona. Yup, I was *that* girl, left with the counselor.

Shimona gave me a pitying smile.

"It's only two days into camp," she said. "It takes time."

My counselor told me the same thing last year.

But I had about as many friends on the last day of camp as I did on the first day. Zero. Or maybe negative two.

"Oh, I almost forgot," Shimona said. "The secretary gave me this phone message for you."

She handed me a piece of paper.

Just checking to see how you're managing without Herman. Love you! Mom and Dad

I glanced at Shimona, hoping she hadn't peeked at the note. *Herman* was our code word for my medication. See, going to sleepaway camp last year had been complicated. I hadn't wanted to take my medication during the summer because it makes me feel like I'm being invaded by an alien version of Lila. An hour after I take a pill, I get so quiet you start wondering if my volume knob is turned all the way down. Hard to imagine! Boy—the looks my parents and Dr. Donut gave me when they considered me going a whole summer without medication.

"We can't risk it, Lila," they'd said.

That's probably because on weekends I don't take my meds, and my parents say I have them running up the walls after me. Which is silly, because I'm not a spider or a fly. Although I did once swing from the chandelier (So. Much. Fun.), I've never climbed the walls.

So at Camp Reyut, I stayed on my meds all summer. Instead of doing camp stuff, all I did was read all day. Not that I don't love reading! It's my favorite activity. But nobody wants to be friends with a book. When the meds wore off in the evenings, everyone was curled up in their sleeping bags, while I was ready to race across campus. That's probably how the rumor started that I was a vampire. Some people in different bunkhouses even pushed beds across their doorways at night to keep me out.

I'm not anti meds. In school they helped me to concentrate, and I was grateful for them. But at camp, meds made me the loneliest girl in the universe, including faraway planets.

That's why this year everyone had agreed to let me give a medication-free summer a royal try. There were only two ways for someone like me to be: on medication or off of it. That's because I have ADHD, which stands for attention deficit hyperactivity disorder. My parents didn't like that name, so I renamed it LWBTCI, which stands for Lila's Wonky Brain That Creates Issues. My parents liked that one even less, so they coined it LECFB for Lila's Extra-Creative Fun Brain. Still, as cool as they were about everything, I knew they were really worried about how things would work out for me without Herman.

"Thanks," I said to Shimona, tucking the note under my pillow.

I followed her through the screen door and walked down the three wooden steps onto the wet grass, which scrunched beneath my patent leather Shabbat shoes. We followed a dirt path that ran between an arch of trees whose leaves rustled in the breeze. The lake spread out in front of us; gray, shimmering, and surrounded by forest. Rows of benches were set up lakeside.

"Girls to the right, boys to the left," our head counselor, Risa, called at the top of her lungs. She usually spoke through a megaphone, and she looked lost without it since we didn't use megaphones on Shabbat. The benches were flanked by overturned canoes and bright orange oars. I breathed in the sweet air and the peacefulness of Shabbat, the Jewish day of rest.

"Slide in next to Esmé," Shimona whispered. Campers were coming by the dozens. I watched them emerging from the trees, everyone wearing their Shabbat clothing.

"Shabbat shalom," I said to Esmé.

She smiled, making me feel encouraged.

"Your outfit's really nice," I said.

"Thanks. It was expensive but worth it."

"It's the color of grass. I like green."

"Me too."

"It's also the color of snot."

Esmé made a face.

I kicked my left foot with my right foot. *Why do I say all these dumb things?* Mom tells me not to be hard on myself, that everyone has their pekalach, meaning they have their own special bag of problems, but somehow none are as neon as mine.

"Not that you need to think about snot just because you're wearing a green dress," I said. "Someone wearing a red dress doesn't need to think about bleeding, right?"

*Foot-in-mouth alert! Removal device necessary!*

Esmé turned to Sarah. "You know, for a second I thought she was giving me a regular compliment."

"Sorry," I said, shaking my head. "Sometimes I—" There were so many things I wanted to say, but they were jumbled up inside me like a giant knot I couldn't untangle. "I really do like your dress."

"Thanks," Sarah said, answering for Esmé the way friends sometimes do.

The benches filled up as the sun began to drop behind the water. The lake was so still, it looked like a flat pancake, and the sun was golden syrup poured over it.

Sarah leaned over and smacked the back of a canoe, making a pinging sound.

"We'll win the canoe race this year," she said.

"What canoe race?" I asked.

"Whoa," Esmé said. "I didn't know anyone at Mah Tovu could not know about the canoe race. At the end of the month, there's color war—you know, your regular three-day, two-team competition—except at Mah Tovu it lasts for a full week. Our teams are always blue and white like the Israeli flag. Anyway, our division's biggest-point activity is the canoe race. Last year, our bunk was on the white team, and we lost the race. That's why our team lost color war."

"Yeah," Sarah said. "This year we're going to win." She flexed her bicep. "Got to build these up so we can paddle hard." She smiled at me. "Are you good at canoeing?"

No. This morning had been my first time canoeing, and I'd nearly fallen out of the canoe and became fish food. Thankfully, I'd been the last canoe in the line, and I was sitting with Shimona, so nobody had noticed.

That's what I *wanted* to say, but the lie swelled in my belly, and I belched it out.

"Yeah, I practiced all summer long at Camp Reyut last year."

"Amazing," Sarah said brightly. "So you'll be great to have on our team. We can all practice on Sunday."

They believed me. Dumb Lila. Unlike the horse-riding lie, this one was going to be discovered in less than forty-eight hours.

Esmé squinted at me. My heart slammed around my ribcage. I was afraid it might slip through and fall onto the ground between us.

"Unfortunately for you," she said, "I saw you nearly fall out of your canoe today. It's obvious you have no canoeing experience. Lying about that could cost our bunk color war. Some of us have been coming to this camp for years and still haven't won a color war. You've already cost our bunk points for cleanup; now you want to ruin the canoe race?"

The air felt prickly as things shifted between me and the rest of the girls, who were listening in. Esmé was right about the canoeing. She was right about cleanup, too. Bunk inspection started on the first day of camp, and the points added up all summer long, going toward whichever team your bunk was on during color war. I wasn't exactly the neatest kid. The girls had asked me to make my bed and put my clothing away this morning, but I'd been distracted by a daddy longlegs trying to crawl across a crack in the bunk floor.

"Oh!" I lied. "I didn't know cleanup counted toward color war."

"And you didn't know about the canoe race, either?" Esmé asked. "Seriously? Did you look at the camp's website before you came here? Did you read the stuff they sent in the mail?"

Sweat gathered like a little river running down my back. I knew about color war and bunk inspections, but I really hadn't known about the canoe race. My mind got all mushy when lies and truth mixed together, like a gross-tasting stew.

"I really am a good canoer. Unfortunately, I got a shoulder injury recently when I uh . . . fell off my horse." I stretched my shoulder, trying to give a convincing wince, though I may have just looked constipated.

"Rrrriiiight," Esmé said. "So what jump were you doing when you fell?" Esmé's eyes were shooting something dangerous—maybe poisonous gas or tiny needles with dangerous chemicals inside.

"No jump," I said. "We were running."

"Running?" she said. "Is that what you call it

when a horse goes very fast?"

Oh man. I knew there was another name for it. I'd even devoured a bunch of horse books, but it was like every word I'd learned since birth, except the word *liar*, had scampered out of my brain.

"You know, I feel like people should be given the option of making up their own dictionaries. My horse was fillyburping. You like that one? It has the word *filly* in it!"

The chazan approached the bimah. Prayers were about to begin. I fiddled with my siddur.

"Do you want to know what I think?" Esmé said.

I did *not* want to know.

"I think you're a fake, Lila Grossberg." She said it loud enough that Becky, Jilly, and the rest of the girls heard. "I think you're lying—about being an equestrian, about being a canoer, and about who knows what else. You only think about yourself and not about the consequences of what you say."

"Uh—maybe my horse was doopaloopading?" I said quietly.

"I think I know all the horse words," Esmé said. "We have stables on our property, and unlike you, I really know how to ride."

Then she turned her back on me as prayers started. Which was a good thing because I needed a miracle to save me.

I'd always been the sort to make deals with God. Things like—if I make it to the end of the swimming pool holding my breath the whole way, then I'll know He's listening to me; and if I make it through the next two hours without saying something dumb as nails, I'll say my prayers every day. Stuff like that.

So I closed my eyes.

*Uh, God, if you could just rewind time three days and let me start over, I'll give all my canteen money to charity.*

I kept my eyes squeezed tight for another minute, but when I opened them, I saw the dark shadow of the lake in the distance and felt the anger of the girls bubbling around me.

*Thanks a lot, God.*

Well, at least I still had my canteen money.

# Chapter 3
## Left Behind

I held the bat between my palms, swinging it around a few times, trying to look professional. There were two outs, so my team was counting on me.

*Come on, arms. Don't let me down.*

*Whack!* I watched the ball spin across the pitcher's mound, bouncing into the outfield like a white marshmallow.

"Run, Lila!" Jilly shouted, snapping me back to life. I ran for first base as a girl from our parallel bunk fielded the ball, throwing it to Becky on first. I skidded to the base just in time. I looked back at the dugout. Esmé, Sarah, Marley, and Ariella were whispering again.

They'd whispered at the table in the dining room during breakfast.

During volleyball. At lunch. During rest hour. At the canteen.

And now.

I bet if someone gathered up all the whispers, they'd be as loud as the PA system that blasts the morning prayer Modeh Ani.

"What's going on?" I asked Becky as I danced onto first base, then off the base, then on it again.

She shrugged. "Dunno."

Ever since Friday night at the lake, nearly a week ago, people tended to answer my questions in sound bites instead of full-length sentences.

"Could you quit moving?" she said.

Ariella struck out, and we headed back to the bunks to get ready for dinner.

There were more whispers over dinner, but I chalked that up to having sloppy joes with many unidentified items in them, so nobody was eating. I was busy making a mound of all the gross-looking things in the sloppy joes on the table. Then I stuck a fork in it, like planting a flag on the moon.

"Ewww," Esmé said.

Later, after night activity, we got back to the bunk, and Sarah said to Esmé, "Let's call it an early night." It had been a pretty exhausting game of capture the flag, so it wasn't *that* weird. Shimona was on her day off, so I didn't even engage in my weird nightly ritual of saying good night to her like she was my substitute mom.

I hopped into bed, snuggled up with my lucky

toucan, and closed my eyes.

⤳

I sat up, blinking. I looked at the numbers glowing on the alarm clock on my nightstand. 3:00 a.m.

I could have sworn I'd heard the screen door slam. I looked toward the door, but it was shut. I closed my eyes and flopped back onto my pillow.

But I couldn't sleep. Something felt . . . odd. It was quiet. Like, outer-space quiet. None of the nighttime snuffling I was used to in the bunkhouse. I looked at Esmé's bed. The moon shone on the blown-up picture of a horse she had on the wall above her bed. I looked at Jilly's bed. She usually slept without a blanket. Not now. She was covered, head to toe.

I stepped out of bed, slipping on my leopard slippers before touching her lightly. I didn't want to wake her. The last thing I needed was for her to like me even less than she already did. I looked around.

Everyone in the bunk was sleeping deep under their covers except for Shimona, who was snoring. Now I was suspicious. I yanked the covers off of Jilly, revealing a giant pile of clothing. I raced over to Becky's bed and pulled back her Girl Power blanket. No Becky, just the contents of her cubbies.

I sat on my bed, feeling it sag. *Where are they?* I peered under the beds. Under Esmé's bed was an empty twenty-four-roll package of toilet paper.

I didn't need more evidence. The pinch in my heart told me everything I needed to know. They'd gone on a raid to TP a bunk on the boys' campus, and they'd left me behind.

Lila Grossberg. Outcast. Loser. Girl who put her foot in her mouth, got it stuck there, walked around with toes poking out of her nose, and nobody ever spoke to her again.

I sat on my bed, squeezing my toucan and feeling

sorry for myself, until a different feeling came over me. I was mad! It was better than sad. Sad was like salt. Mad was like a spicy pepper. Who doesn't like a generous dash of hot sauce on their food?

Now what?

I paced, the wooden floorboards creaking under my leopard-print slippers. For two seconds, I considered waking Shimona and tattling, but that would only make things worse for me. Then I'd be a *rat*. Besides, even Lila Grossberg had boundaries (very flexible ones). So what *would* I do?

I had it! I wasn't invited, but I had every right to go join their raid. I could imagine the looks on their faces when they'd see brave Lila, who had crossed the woods alone in the middle of the night. I was so stoked, I ran out of the bunk, the door slamming shut behind me. It was dark, with only a tiny slice of moon like a dangling bulb in the sky. Fog clogged the girls' campus. Crickets chirped, and in the distance, I heard the *clickety clack* of a tractor.

I walked to the edge of the bunkhouses until the dirt path appeared. Right took me to the lake. Left took me to the road that curled around the main camp and led to the boys' campus. It was cold, but I was sweating. I broke into a run. What if I got there and they were already gone? I'd feel smaller than an atom on a molecule on a flea on a puppy. I ran and ran, my breath the loudest sound around. Finally, the fog cleared, and I could make out the trees, like hooded, many-limbed creatures, the kind you don't want to hang out with. The bit of moon gave enough light that I could see I wasn't anywhere near the boys' campus. I must have made a wrong turn, but where was I now?

I suddenly remembered how the kids in my class had once placed a dead frog in my lunch box, and

I'd come home crying. My mother had frowned and said, "Lila, I'm calling the teacher about their behavior. This is really the last straw." Well, now I felt like the girls leaving me behind had been the last straw, and getting lost while trying to find them was like someone had crumpled up the straw box and tossed it into the trash.

I leaned against the closest tree and slid to the ground, not caring that I was sitting on prickly fir needles or that the ground was wet with dew. I wrapped my hands around my knees, shivering.

*God. Help me fix all this.*

I couldn't think of anything to offer in return.

That's when I heard a crackling, like the crunch of grass, leaves, and pine cones.

I looked up, and there it was.

A horse.

# Chapter 4
## I Met a Horse!

She was standing about twenty feet away from me in the clearing, her head slightly cocked, as if asking a question. She was brown, with white spots running down the length of her face and at the bottom of her front legs but nowhere else that I could see. She was shiny, like a brand-new car. I stood up quickly, and she took a step backward.

Okay, she didn't like that.

We stood, staring at each other. I took one tiny

step toward her. She took one horse step back.

*Think, Lila, think. What do horses like?*

Sugar cubes. That's what horses in stories always liked. I reached for my pocket, realizing I was wearing Mario pajamas that had no pockets.

Seriously? I was planning on showing up to the boys' campus in Mario pajamas? I may as well have dressed up as a gorilla wearing a kayak as a hat.

I looked into the horse's giant brown eyes. She blinked. I blinked.

"Could you take me back to my bunk?" I asked. I imagined how awesome that would be. The girls would be coming back from the raid, and I'd parade in on horseback. I'd be an instant celebrity. If there were a road paved with stars in Mah Tovu like the one they had in Hollywood, my name would be next to the four-time canoe-race winner.

She shook her head right and left, like she was

saying no, although she was probably getting rid of a fly. She whinnied, then stepped in a circle, turning her huge body around. She trotted back to the woods. Trot! Gallop! Canter! All horse words! I was a horseatarian! Not that it helped me now.

"Wait!" I called out after her.

She didn't turn back. I watched until the trees swallowed her up.

I wasn't one to take a sign for granted. She'd been sent for me. But now, I had to get back to the bunk. I retraced my steps, finding my way back to the girls' campus. I barged into the bunk to find everyone there and very much awake—even Shimona.

"These eyes do not see, these ears don't hear," Shimona said. "I should report you all for using all that toilet paper." But she was smiling. She looked up over everyone's heads.

"Hey, Lila," she said. "Did you get lost coming back?"

Everyone fell silent. A silence so big and hard, you could stub your toe on it.

I could have ratted them out for leaving me behind. But I thought of the horse's wise eyes.

"Uh, yeah, I got lost," I said. "But I met a horse! In the woods! It was wild, uh, I mean, no saddle or muzzle or anything. And horses—they gallop, by the way. Or canter. Or trot!"

"You met a horse in the woods?" Esmé said, her voice sounding like she'd scooped it out of a pot of sarcastic stew.

"Yeah. She's gorgeous. If she's a she. I think she is. She wouldn't let me approach. She looked . . . I don't know, scared?"

"Right," Becky said.

"Uh-huh," Jilly said.

Sarah met my eyes, then looked away.

"Also," Esmé said, using the same tone as before,

"I'm not really a person. I'm a pig. Which means I'm not kosher. Uh-oh."

"Esmé, that's enough," Shimona said.

"What?" Esmé said, hands on her hips. "Do you believe her? She lied about having experience with horses, and now we're supposed to buy that she's solved the legend of Camp Mah Tovu's wild horses? Besides, if she knew horses, she'd know wild horses don't hang by themselves. Where was its herd?"

"Come back to the woods with me," I said. "You'll see for yourselves."

Esmé shook her head like I wasn't even worth this conversation.

I looked to Marley for support—she was the nicest of the bunch—but her mouth was set in an angry line. I glanced up at Shimona, on the top bunk.

"We should all get some sleep," she said. "We can

talk more in the morning."

Even *she* didn't believe me.

I looked at Sarah again. This time she met my eyes and held them.

Mom says eyes are the windows to the soul. Looking through Sarah's eye-windows, here's what I saw:

*I believe you, Lila.*

It gave me something to hang my hat on, if I had been holding a hat.

"Give me a chance," I said. "Come with me to the woods tomorrow. I'll show her to you."

Esmé eyed me. She looked at Sarah, then up at the picture of the horse hanging over her bed.

"Okay," she said.

# Chapter 5
## Say Hello to Lonny

In the morning, after prayers, our bunk had cleanup. I never understood the point of cleaning up. Things got messy again five minutes later. At home, when my mother asked me to straighten up, I'd stuff everything under my blanket. Voilà! Clean as a whistle. I knew the girls wanted me to clean so they could get their dumb points, but I had places to go, animals to see! I needed to retrace my steps from last night. I prayed my horse would still be there so

I could show her to the girls. Then they'd definitely want to be my friends. Just to be helpful, though, I shoved my mess under my blanket.

I stopped by the woodshop on my way. Talia, the shop counselor, was clearing bits of leather off the table when I arrived. Talia was a legend at Mah Tovu. Everyone loved her, from the tip of her curly red hair to the bottoms of her black rubber waders. Today her hair looked wild, like she'd stuck her finger in a socket, then put mousse in to make it stay that way.

"Hey, Lila," she said, smiling big. Mom tells me I'm good at figuring out whether a smile comes from a person's mouth or from a person's heart. Talia had a heart smile. "How can I help you?"

"Uh, I need a length of rope."

She wiped her hands on her apron. "Sure thing. What for?"

I didn't want to tell Talia about the horse. She'd tell me it was dangerous and put a stop to my plan.

"So, our bunk is making a ropes course. Also, I like to jump rope." I considered adding a third thing involving tying a couch to the top of a car but figured it might make her suspicious.

She swung a cabinet open and began unraveling a length of rope from a thick metal spool.

"This ought to do it," she said, handing it to me.

I nodded and backed toward the door.

"And Lila," she said as I pushed the door open with my thigh.

"Yeah?"

"If you need anything else, I'm around."

"Sure," I said. "I'm also around."

*I'm also around? What did I just say?*

I have a good sense of direction when it isn't dark and foggy, so I repeated all the wrong turns I'd made last night until I arrived in the clearing where I'd met the horse. She wasn't there.

"Horse!" I cried at the top of my lungs.

I heard nothing.

"Hoooooorrrrrrssssse."

No response.

Maybe the horse didn't appreciate being called by such an impersonal title. I had to name her.

I tossed a bunch of names around in my head.

*Sparky? Sounds like a dog.*

*Buffalo? That will give it an identity crisis.*

*Chestnut? Her and a million other horses.*

And then it came to me. What had Esmé said? That wild horses always hung with their herds?

My horse was a loner.

Just like me.

"Loner!" I cried at the top of my lungs. But that name sounded too pathetic. I needed to change it up a bit. "Lonny!" I cried.

I heard the crunch of leaves. I broke into a smile when I saw her brown-and-white face.

"Hey!" I said.

She stood about twenty feet away from me. I held the rope out like I was offering her a delicious meal, then I slowly tied a knot, making a lasso. Thankfully, I'd spent a summer with my family on my uncle's farm in the Catskills. There hadn't been any horses there, but I'd helped him lasso plenty of goats.

All I needed was a cowboy hat. (I still didn't have a hat, but at least I wasn't wearing pajamas.)

I held out the rope.

"I'm going to, uh, catch you so I can keep you here, just for a bit. I need to prove that you're real. It'll help me out a lot. Then I'll let you go. Promise."

I was scared she'd bolt before I had a chance to secure her. I waved the rope over my head. Lonny snorted and pinned her ears back. I could tell she was about to run, but the rope caught around her neck before she could. I quickly pulled it, tying the end around the tree. Lonny kicked and strained.

"Sorry!" I said. She moved her head left to right. I wanted to comfort her, but I had no time. I raced back through the woods, past the dining room and the swimming pool, down the row of bunkhouses until I reached mine. Panting, I blew inside.

"You coming to see my horse?" I asked the girls.

Esmé looked at Sarah.

"Now it's *your* horse?" she said. But she motioned to Sarah. "Come on, let's go."

Esmé and Sarah followed as I ran back the same way I'd come, with the two of them at my heels.

"You're going to love her," I called over my shoulder.

We arrived at the clearing where Lonny was.

43

"Here she is!" I shouted triumphantly.

Where Lonny *wasn't*.

She was gone. The busted lasso lay on the ground.

"Hey, look," Esmé said. "It *is* a ghost horse!"

"Yeah," Sarah said. "Or maybe an invisible horse."

I turned sharply toward Sarah, but she was looking straight at Esmé.

Esmé snapped her fingers, like she was making an important decision.

"We have to get ready for swim," she said. "The canoe test is today. We don't have any more time for your games, Lila."

Esmé left, followed by Sarah. I didn't have the heart to do anything. Not only had I let them down, I'd let Lonny down, too. She'd never get within spitting distance of me after what I did to her today.

I had no idea how to fix things with Lonny or my bunkmates, but I figured it was easier to patch things up with a horse than with people. I raced back to camp and banged on the woodshop door. One of the younger bunk groups was inside, and Talia was gluing birdhouses with them. She looked up. Her goggles made her look like an astronaut.

"You said that you could help me?" I asked her.

She nodded. "Sure thing, Lila."

"So, uh, what do you know about wild horses?"

She smiled as she set a birdhouse down, and a little kid grabbed it back.

"Just call me Horses 'R' Us. I've been doing the horse life for two decades now. I'm a woodshop instructor by summer, and a horse whisperer during the fall, winter, and spring. And by the way, I didn't buy your ropes-course lie. Now let's get started. We have a lot of work to do."

# Chapter 6
## Sweeble School

"Are you sure you're okay missing night activity?" Talia asked me as we sat on the grass in the woods, waiting for Lonny. I hadn't seen Lonny in three days, but Talia and I had been busy in the computer room. I'd learned that wild horses are also called mustangs and that they were considered a symbol of the American frontier. I'd *read* about how to lead a horse. Now I had to figure out how to actually *do* it.

"There's a pie-making contest tonight," I said.

"Me, my bunkmates, and pies? I'd have pie all over my face, trust me."

Talia laughed. "That bad, eh?"

"Worse."

I thought back to my phone call to my parents yesterday morning. Risa had given me special permission to call home, as my parents had already left three messages about "Herman." Risa was convinced I had a sick great-uncle or something. I'd spent the entire conversation convincing my parents that camp was amazing, stupendous, fabulous, and every other adjective that would make it seem like things were going great with me off of my meds. The truth was far from it, but I did *not* want to get my parents involved. When that kid at school had left a frog in my knapsack, Mom had insisted on stepping in. Everyone called me "Mama's girl" for like six months after that, and things didn't get even an inch better. I was *not* doing that again.

My pockets were stuffed with Shugabirds. I nibbled on one. I couldn't sit still. I jumped up.

It was dark, with a smudge of moon lighting the forest. I walked in a circle, touching the trees like I was getting to know them.

"Hello, knotty one," I said.

"Hey, gnarly guy."

There was a tree with a hole in the bark, probably where some animal had camped. I wished I could snuggle up inside. I decided it was my favorite tree.

"Much as I'd love to sleep here under the stars, Lila," Talia said, "we need a good chunk of time with this horse of yours, so it better get here quick."

*Bring me back my horse, God. Please give me one more chance. I'll stop lying. Really.*

I wondered if that was a lie.

"Lonny!"

"Resist the urge to shout," whispered Talia. "Let's be as quiet as these woods."

We waited. I must have dozed off because I felt Talia shaking me awake. Her hair under the moonlight looked like a bonfire.

"She's right there," Talia whispered. "You're correct, by the way. It's a she."

I blinked the sleep from my eyes. There she was.

I stood and brushed the pine needles off my shirt. I took one baby step forward. Her head snapped up.

"You're angry with me," I said. "I know."

I didn't walk any closer, and I didn't look her in the eye, just like Talia had taught me. I walked right, then left, zigging and zagging playfully, just like the videos Talia had shown me. Lonny stayed put. I reached into my pocket, feeling for a Shugabird.

I swerved left, then right, slowly, slowly, only coming just a tiny bit closer.

"Hey," I said when I was ten feet away from her. "I'm sorry for spooking you the other day. I was using you to impress my bunkmates. Forgive me? Please?"

I took a step closer, then another. Slow and steady until, finally, I was within arm's reach.

"Don't scoot," I said. I offered up a Shugabird. I would have given her more, but Talia said they weren't really healthy for her.

"These are my favorites," I said. "But I want to share them with you."

I looked back at Talia, standing about three feet behind me. She nodded and smiled.

Lonny dipped her head, slowly, into my palm. I felt her nose, soft and warm, then her lips, wet and rubbery. I looked at my hand. The Shugabird was gone!

"Thanks for forgiving me," I said softly. She began to walk, and I walked alongside her, keeping a safe distance between us.

"Let's get the halter on her," Talia said. "Leave this part to me. Watch and learn."

Talia spent some time introducing Lonny to the halter. Then she slipped it expertly over Lonny's head and clipped a lead to it. She handed me the end of the lead.

"Walk her in circles. I'm right next to you."

"But I want to ride her!"

"Oh, you do?" Talia said, laughing. "What did I tell you about breaking the horse? You know, I don't even like that term. Who wants to break a horse? Or any animal for that matter?"

"Not me."

"Me neither," Talia said. "How about we make up our own word?"

I couldn't believe Talia also made up words! I had a whole notebook of them back home. Like *vacootator*, which is a tiny vacuum cleaner with a blade that also cuts vegetables. It doesn't really exist, but it would be cool.

"How about we're sweebling the horse?" I said.

"Oh yes," Talia said. "I've sweebled many horses in the past. Some horses are more sweebable than others. This horse looks especially sweebleworthy, don't you think?"

"Definitely," I said. The moment felt so magical, I didn't need to say anything more.

I took hold of the lead, basically a rope attached to the halter, stood off to Lonny's side, and followed Talia's commands, gently tugging Lonny's head in my direction. It was like trying to move a pile of bricks with a feather. I kept trying until, finally, she turned her head a bit toward me. I immediately released my grip, giving her reinforcement.

"Amazing," Talia cried.

I barely even noticed Talia. It felt like Lonny and I were the only two people in the universe. Yeah, I knew Lonny wasn't a person, but it didn't seem like there was enough standing between us to put us in *totally* different categories.

"Good girl!" I said. I kept up my work, tugging and releasing the lead when she did what I wanted. She was learning. We stayed there for three hours. Three hours when I wasn't thinking about anything else—not mean Esmé or any of the other girls who thought I was the biggest pain in North Carolina.

"Okay," Talia called out. "As besweebled as I am by what you've accomplished this evening, we need to get back to camp, or Shimona will send me to the guillotine. That refers to an ancient beheading device, in case you didn't know."

"I know," I said. "I read a lot." My parents told me the reason my brain always vomited information was because it had so much stuff crammed in there, it needed to make space for more.

"Well, not enough about horses, apparently," she said. "Which is a good thing. I don't fancy being useless."

That got me to look away from Lonny for just a second. I wondered if Talia really worried about things like that. She was probably the most popular person in the whole camp. Everyone knew that when she was in charge of any activity, it was bound to be fun. Girls said that whichever team got Talia for color war was the surest one to win.

"Give me back the lead," Talia said. Then she took the halter off of Lonny.

"When do I get to ride her?"

"You're nearly as impatient as I am, and that's a big stack of impatience. Riding is an art, not a science. You're a natural, but you've still got a lot of sweeble school to attend. We'll continue tomorrow."

"When?"

"After breakfast?"

"And?"

"After lunch?"

"And?" I asked as I handed the lead to Talia.

"While you're sleeping?" she said. "They say babies absorb information if you play it to them while they're asleep. We could try that."

I laughed. "Goodbye, my friend," I said to Lonny.

She gave me one last look, then lowered her head to graze.

"Aw," Talia said. "She's probably the weakest in the herd, and there isn't enough grazing land for everyone. That's why she comes out here to eat. Her herd is nearby, I'm sure of it."

Lonny was left out of everything, just like me.

"Let's skedaddle," Talia said.

We walked across the clearing, back through the trees, emerging on the girls' campus.

"Toodle-oo!" Talia called, giving me a little wave. I couldn't believe my luck. Why was Talia being so nice to me?

I started running toward my bunk.

"Excuse me!" said a loud voice.

Uh-oh. It was Risa, speaking through her megaphone, even though she was standing a few feet away from me. "Why are you not in your bunk sleeping, Lila Grossberg?"

"Uh," I said. But she was already flipping through the camp handbook that she carried with her everywhere she went. "Gallivanting at night without a counselor violates rule number three twenty-six."

"I-I was with Talia," I said.

Risa put her hands on her hips. "Well then. I'll check with her on that. But I have my eye on you."

*Phew!* I raced the rest of the way back to the bunk. A few of the girls were still awake.

"You missed a great night activity," Marley said. She really was nice.

"Yeah, thanks." I had a lot of things I wanted to tell her, like: *I have a horse! Her name is Lonny! I'm taming her!*

But I knew there was no hope of anyone believing me unless I rode her right into camp. I'd considered asking Talia to inform the girls that I was telling the truth, but needing a counselor to stick up for me would make me an even bigger loser than I already was. Like the last time my mother had gotten involved in my drama. I'd even thought of figuring out a way to take pictures of Lonny to show everyone, but they'd just think I'd photoshopped them or something. They'd made up their minds about me. It was too late.

Somehow, though, that felt okay. So long as *I* knew Lonny was real, that was enough for now.

∽

The next day, during rest period, I went to meet Talia in the computer room. She wasn't there, so I continued researching on my own. I was getting Lonny to trust me, but I needed to take it to the next level. I wanted to ride her. For that, I needed a saddle. Talia was definitely the right person to help me. She was the type who could build a city that would last forever out of disposable plastic cups.

I was reading up on how to get a wild horse to let you saddle it when I heard someone speaking. The computer room had two stations with a nearly ceiling-high partition built between them. I was sitting at the inside computer, and there was no way anyone could have known I was there without checking.

I recognized her voice right away. It was Sarah, on the computer next to mine.

"H-h-o-pful," Sarah said.

I waited to hear her voice again. Finally, she said, "Toodle?"

Then it sounded like she threw something. I looked down and saw a pair of headphones on the floor.

"Try again!" the computer said in a cheerful voice.

"Toodle!" Sarah shouted. "I told you, it's toodle!"

"That is not correct," the computer said, sounding way too cheerful for telling someone they'd gotten the wrong answer. "Try again!"

"I don't want to try again," Sarah muttered.

I sat, frozen, listening as the computer asked Sarah to read a few more words and she kept missing the boat. I didn't know what to do. Clearly, she thought the room was empty. I could have made a noise, like *garumph!* Or blown my nose, which always made me sound like a train's whistle. Or slid my foot under the partition, but it probably would have gotten stuck there, and then she'd have to call the maintenance man to come take apart the partition to get me out. Or they'd have to take me to the hospital along with the partition, and they'd have to load me and the partition onto a pickup truck, and the whole camp would watch me being carted out that way. Any of those options would lead to her knowing that it was Lila Grossberg sitting next to her in the computer room. She'd know I'd figured out she had trouble reading. Mom says it's never good to know too much about someone else's kishkes—all that icky stuff roiling around inside of them. On the other hand, telling her that I knew might make her feel less alone.

*HAAAAA!!!!! As if she really wants Lila Grossberg's emotional support.* I'd probably say twenty dumb things like:

"Hey! You can't read, so you'll never have to read a bad book."

Or "I couldn't read either, when I was one year old."

Or "Reading is totally overrated; now, horses are a different story."

So I figured I ought to shut it.

I stayed as quiet as a droplet falling on really poufy grass, listening to her struggle until, finally, she sighed loudly and left the computer room, slamming the door behind her.

I guess it's true that everyone has their pekalach.

# Chapter 7
## The Herd

I woke up feeling lousy inside. Talia got ahold of a saddle, and I'd been trying to saddle Lonny under her guidance for more than a week already. Every time I thought I was making progress, Lonny bolted so far, I was afraid she'd end up in California.

I stumbled to the showers wearing my Betty Boop robe. Both showers were taken, and Esmé was in line before me. She was holding a basket of shower stuff. I counted seven different bottles as I hopped from one foot to the other.

"Whoa," I said. "Uh, let me guess. Shampoo, conditioner, body wash, uh, milk for your cereal?"

Esmé rolled her eyes. "Face cleanser. Callous softener. Hair mask. Not that you care."

"I care, that's why I asked."

"Nah. You just like to hear yourself talk. Like a parrot."

I felt like someone had punched me in the stomach and their hand had come out the other side of me.

I didn't *like* hearing myself talk. I just *had* to talk. But there was no chance of someone like Esmé understanding. In school, there were a few kids who knew I took medication to help me to concentrate, but they'd known me since I was pea size—so it never felt weird. Every time I considered telling the kids in camp about my "creative" brain, someone like Esmé made a comment so rotten, I got nauseous from the idea.

Marley stepped out of the shower, and Esmé jumped in and flashed me a dirty look before tugging the curtain closed.

"Hey," Marley said.

I smiled wide although I felt like frowning.

"Good morning," I said. "You smell clean."

She stared at me. "Ummm, thanks? I guess?"

"It's a compliment. Trust me. I had a girl in my class this year who smelled weird—like a mixture of moldy fruit and the inside of shoes. When the teacher made people pick partners for projects, she was always the last one to be chosen."

I didn't mention that I was always the second-to-last one to be chosen.

Marley looked right, then left, as if checking that the coast was clear.

"Listen," she said softly. "I think you're nice enough, that's why I'm going to tell you this. But the girls are really mad at you for disappearing during cleanup every morning. We get points taken off for your bed every inspection. Color war is really important around here."

I put my hands on my hips, forgetting I was holding my all-in-one shampoo/conditioner/body wash. It clattered to the floor.

"That's not my fault. Have you seen Jilly's cubbies?"

Marley took a step back. I hoped Esmé couldn't hear us over the sound of the water running.

"Seriously," I continued. "It's not fair to blame everything on me. I'm doing important things with my time. I'm riding my horse!"

This was only a semi lie.

Marley squeezed a glob of toothpaste onto her

toothbrush. "I'm just trying to help. Maybe you should admit that you're doing something wrong instead of dumping the blame."

Esmé stepped out of the shower, glaring.

"Yeah, Lila," she said. "Marley's right."

Well, in case anyone was wondering, shower water is not loud enough to drown out conversations!

"You're ganging up on me," I said, taking a few steps backward, out of the shower room and into the bunk. Marley and Esmé followed.

"She thinks we're ganging up on her," Esmé said to everyone in the bunk. "Is that true?" She whispered something into Jilly's ear.

"Maybe you shouldn't blame things on me," Jilly muttered as she made her bed.

"Maybe you should think about someone other than yourself," Ariella said.

I looked from one bunkmate to another, and I

saw a row of angry faces. There was nobody on my team. Nobody. I thought of Lonny, wandering the dark woods on her own, looking for food.

At least she had the birds flitting around her, the bugs crawling underfoot, and the squirrels scampering through the trees. I was alone with a capital *A*.

I had to go to prayers. I had to go to breakfast. I had to clean up my space before the girls got even madder at me. But I didn't care about any of that now. My heart felt like it had been run through a paper shredder. I raced out of the bunkhouse. Shimona was on the porch, gathering the bathing suits that had been hung to dry.

"Hey!" she cried. "Where are you going?"

I didn't answer. I ran as fast as my legs could carry me toward the woodshop. It was drizzling, but I didn't care about that, either. I pulled on the screen door, but it was locked.

"Talia!" I cried, banging on the door again, even though she obviously wasn't there. If she couldn't help me, I'd do it myself. I backed away from the woodshop and ran down the dirt road, into the woods, through the trees, until I reached the clearing.

"Lonny?" I called.

Nothing.

I sank to the ground and began to cry. Not just a few little tears, either. I sobbed, taking giant gulps of air. It was all my fault that everybody hated me.

"Lonny!" I cried when I didn't have a single tear left inside of me. "I need you!"

And suddenly, there she was—tall and shining, right in front of me.

I stood up slowly, brushing myself off.

"You came?" I said.

She whinnied as if to say, *"Yes. I came. For you."*

I reached out and gently touched her on the side of her head. She felt smooth, like those plastic chairs at the airport I'd sat in a few weeks ago, leaving for camp.

"Lonny," I said softly. "Will you let me ride you?"

She stood still as a stone. I backed away and looked for the tree where Talia had hung the halter and saddle. I lifted them and dragged the saddle on the ground toward Lonny.

"I'm just going to lay this on your back so you can carry me," I told her. "Then we can ride like the wind. Okay?"

She looked at me, her brown eyes wide and wise.

I let her sniff and bite the halter, just like I'd seen Talia do, and then I buckled it on her. It was as easy as brushing my teeth when I haven't eaten spinach that gets stuck in every tooth. Then I waited. She stood as still as a parked car, and I waited some more. I lifted the saddle high. It nearly bowled me over. I could just imagine the local news tomorrow: Girl trampled . . . not by horse—but by its saddle! How was I going to get this on Lonny's back? I needed a stool.

*Uh, hey, God, you brought me this far, could I have a stool, please?*

I scanned the clearing. Then it occurred to me—this was a clearing. The area had been cleared by loggers. The edge of the clearing was dotted with tree stumps. Otherwise known as—stools! I lay the saddle on the ground. I just needed to get Lonny to walk toward a stump.

Sure! Just get a thousand-pound horse to move. Like, excuse me, mountain that's been standing here for thousands of years, but would you mind moving over *there*?

I thought back to some of the stuff that Talia and

I had read together over the past few weeks.

"Come on," I said, concentrating with all my might, trying to connect my heart with Lonny's. I tugged on the rope, and she turned around! I released, leading her as she walked behind me. As we approached the tree stumps, I realized I had no idea how to get her to stop. Talia and I hadn't gotten that far. I'd just have to keep walking her through this forest and then the next one. We'd probably end up in Wyoming.

But magically, Lonny stopped when I did.

"Good girl," I said. I leaned my cheek against the side of her face. She felt like velvet and chocolate and the most comfortable shirt you've ever worn.

"Wait here," I said.

I walked back slowly to pick up the saddle, taking care not to step behind her. I dragged the saddle back to Lonny and climbed on a stump, holding the saddle across my arms like some weird offering.

"I'm just going to lay this on your back," I said. "It's not scary."

As if she understood, she took a step toward me. But as I came toward her, she bucked.

I tried approaching again, but this time she bucked before I got within five feet of her.

"What? You don't want to be my friend? Fine! You'll have to get in line, though."

Lonny looked at me with her warm, brown eyes, and I knew that it wasn't true. She wasn't going to let me ride her. But she was my friend.

I sighed.

"Okay. We'll just walk then."

I hopped off of the stump and took hold of the lead. I wanted to be gentle, but I knew I needed to be firm. Lonny was beautiful and kind, but she could be dangerous if I didn't handle her right. I led her into the forest, away from camp. Rain began to fall, and her hooves squished through the waterlogged grass. I could see where the earth was flattened, creating a path through the trees, and I got excited, thinking this must be the trail Lonny took every day to get to the clearing. If I followed it, maybe we'd reach her herd.

Normally, it's hard for me to take long walks without skipping or breaking into a run. But with Lonny beside me, I had to be careful and steady.

We came to a small stream, and I walked her over to it, resting my weary feet and letting her drink. She took big gulps of water. Then she looked at me like she was waiting for me to tell her what to do. Little old me! I kept on following the trail with her until the trees narrowed together, then widened into a huge clearing that looked like marshland.

I stopped, and Lonny stopped beside me. My

breath caught in my throat. There, in the meadow, separated from us by a tall fringe of brush, were wild horses. They were almost all brown like Lonny, but some had more white and some had no white at all. They were shiny with rain. There were twelve in all, including three foals. And I don't know why, but the sight of them made me tear up again.

"That's your family?" I finally said.

Lonny snorted.

So this was like Lonny's camp bunk.

I heard a strange rumbling in the sky, but it didn't sound like thunder. It sounded like a giant wearing clogs was thumping across the clouds. The sound got closer, and I could sense the fear rising off Lonny's back the way steam comes out of street vents. Something was happening. I didn't know what it was, but I knew I wasn't experienced enough to handle an agitated horse on my own. I took off

Lonny's halter, hoping she'd run to join her herd, but she stayed next to me, whinnying.

The sounds grew louder, and all the horses in the meadow began to whinny and jostle around. The foals moved near their mothers. It was dangerous for me to stand next to Lonny, but I couldn't abandon her when she was afraid.

Then a helicopter dropped beneath a gray cloud, its blades furiously whipping the air. The horses in the field raced to and fro, their terror obvious. Without any warning, Lonny bucked. Her right flank bumped me, not enough to hurt me but hard enough that I lost my balance and tumbled to the ground, landing on my arm. I lay on the ground, stunned, while Lonny ran off.

The helicopter dropped a bit lower. I hoisted myself up, holding my throbbing left wrist with my right hand. Suddenly I saw a man, chasing the horses with a whip.

*No!*

I could hear him shouting into a device over the *chop-chop-chop* of the helicopter blades.

"Hook right, Dansky!"

The helicopter made a sharp right, dropping lower still. What were they doing?

I heard a rumbling again, and this time it really was thunder. Then a fog spread over the field like spilled milk.

"Too much fog, Dansky," the guy with the whip shouted into whatever device he was holding. "We'll come back." The horses ran, their hoofbeats sounding like drums. I couldn't find Lonny.

The helicopter dropped to the earth, picking up the man with the whip. It lifted back up, making a sharp left turn. Then it rose back into the clouds and its sound became fainter. I watched as it got farther and farther away, until it disappeared.

The horses were still going crazy. I looked at my watch. If I didn't get back to camp, Risa would punish me for infractions numbers 6,270 and 4,089. And if anyone checked with Talia, I'd be fried, since she'd realize I was out with Lonny on my own. She'd report me to the police, and they'd come down to camp, and everyone would think it was an early color war breakout until they realized it was just Lila Grossberg causing trouble again.

"I'll be back," I cried to Lonny as I scampered away, feeling like I'd swallowed a stone and it was stuck halfway down my windpipe.

Lonny and the rest of those horses were in big trouble. I had to figure out what was going on.

# Chapter 8
## An Even Swap

At breakfast, I shoveled a spoonful of farina into my mouth, not even tasting it. Dansky. It was probably just a coincidence that Sarah had the same last name, right? But her father was a rancher, and she was one of the only kids here from North Carolina. How could I get Sarah to talk to me?

"Anyone want anything?" our waitress, Shira, asked.

"Soy milk," Esmé said. Esmé always wanted

*something*. She loved being served.

"And sugar substitute," Esmé added. She put her hands on her hip bones, which were jutting out like hangers. "Watching my weight."

Shira rolled her eyes and went back through the swinging doors of the kitchen.

"You okay, Lila?" Shimona asked. "Cat got your tongue this morning?"

"If a cat ever got hold of *her* tongue," Esmé said, "it would run back and return it. Trust me, Lila can't manage an hour without it, and no cat could stomach it."

"Esmé," Shimona said. "Uncalled for."

I'd been laying low for a couple of days. I was too scared of getting caught if I went back to the forest alone. Thankfully, my wrist was only sprained, but I'd had to concoct a whole crazy story about how it had happened, involving frogs, mice, and a lot of candy (don't ask). I even spun a tale for Talia. I was afraid she'd be furious that I'd gone to see Lonny on my own, and if I got thrown out of camp, there was no way I could help Lonny. All I could think about was that helicopter, those horrible men, and the fear running wild in that field of mustangs.

I'd spent my rest period these past two days in the computer room, hoping Sarah would show up so I could get her alone, but she hadn't. I needed her.

We finished eating, said grace after meals, and brought our bowls and cutlery to the dishes bin.

I managed my way through softball, basketball, arts and crafts, and lunch. Then I raced to the computer room, where I continued looking up information about Lonny and her herd. Apparently, the local ranchers thought the wild herds threatened their animals' grazing land. The government "took care" of the problem, rounding up the horses by intimidating them with helicopters. They corralled them into trailers, separating mothers from their babies, and carted them off to other destinations, where they were sold and often slaughtered—if they survived the journey. Others were cooped up in holding pens for the rest of their lives. Only a lucky few were adopted, but even they never saw their families again. I couldn't understand how anyone could be that cruel.

I sucked on a Shugabird as the door creaked open, and my heart leaped. *Please, God, let it be Sarah!*

Within minutes, I heard her fighting with the computer again. I jumped up and pushed my chair back.

"Hi!" I said loudly, since she was wearing headphones. She didn't hear me, so I jabbed her between the shoulder blades.

"Ow!" Sarah said, turning around.

Oopsie.

"Sorry, I was just trying to get your attention."

She looked at me blankly, and I realized she was still wearing headphones. I lifted them off her head.

"What are you doing?" she said.

Double oopsie.

"Is your father Dansky?" I asked.

Ugh. I was supposed to ease into things slowly. I wanted to gobble back up my words, but it was too late.

"Yeah, I have the same last name as him, so what?" she said.

"Uh, that's not really what I meant." I reached over and switched the light switch off, then on, then off again, then on again. "He's a rancher, right?"

"Yeah. So?"

I thought of all the times Sarah had refused to participate in horse-related bunk talk. She was hiding something. I was sure of it.

"You believe me, don't you? Because you know about the wild horses."

Sarah looked over her shoulder.

"Because you know there are wild horses on Mah Tovu's grounds. And you know that your father is trying to get rid of them."

She shrugged, but I could tell from her eyes that she cared a whole lot more than a shrug.

"And what if that's true? Then what?"

"Then I need you to help me," I said. "Because my horse could be separated from its herd. She could die, Sarah!" I flipped the light switch off again.

"Could you quit doing that?" she cried.

"Is Dansky your father?"

She looked at her shoes. "Yes," she said quietly.

"Well, I need you to help me."

"What on earth do you want *me* to do?"

This was my moment.

"Tonight is Tisha B'av," I said, referring to the Jewish fast day commemorating the destruction of our two holy temples. "Tomorrow, they're taking us off the grounds to hear a Holocaust survivor speak. We can ask Shimona to get us permission to visit with your father."

Sarah shook her head fast.

"Why would I want to speak to my dad about this? If you have a problem, why should I fix it?"

"Because," I said, "this problem belongs to everyone. Besides, I know about your reading issue. You should really check behind dividers more often. Seriously, I could tell you stories about people who—"

Sarah narrowed her eyes. "Are you blackmailing me?"

Now it was my turn to shake my head just as fast

as she had. "No. I wouldn't do that. I know what it's like to have school problems. I have lots of them. But reading happens to be one of the things I'm really good at. Last year, in fourth grade, I was pulled out of class to do seventh-grade reading. Like, reverse resource room. I'm suggesting an even swap. You help me to save the horses. I help you with your reading."

She was quiet. As usual, I ached to fill the quiet with noise, but thinking of Lonny, I managed to zip my lips.

"Who says I need your help?" Sarah asked. "I have tutors. They gave me a computer program to work on during the summer."

"I know," I said. "I was there when you attacked it. I'm glad it's still alive. But maybe it was better off dead. It didn't seem to be helping much."

Sarah sighed and slumped against the wall.

"It's the worst," she said. Her eyes filled with tears. "You're not going to tell anyone, are you?" she asked.

"No way. Not in a million, a billion, or a trillion years. Not even when people start flying, because I'm convinced that will happen one day."

"Thanks. Even Esmé doesn't know, and she's in school with me. The teachers are careful not to call on me to read and stuff. I guess I'm just dumb."

I shook my head really fast. "You're not dumb. No way. Trust me. Do you know what the word *dumb* means?"

Sarah shrugged.

"Temporarily unable or unwilling to speak. I know because I looked it up last summer when kids were calling me dumb because—well, it doesn't matter—you probably can't imagine *me* being unable to talk. But you speak perfectly. And you're *trying*, during summer vacation, which is, like, the opposite of dumb. If anyone's dumb, it's that computer program you're working with. It sounds like it's throwing itself a party every time you get a wrong answer."

Sarah laughed. Then I laughed, which turned into a snort.

"I hope you're a good teacher," Sarah said. "You talk enough to be a teacher."

"Does that mean—"

"Yeah, okay," Sarah said. "I'll call my father. I can't promise you anything, though. He's a tough cookie. That's what my mother says."

I nodded, feeling like I might pop into pieces from happiness.

"I'm coming, Lonny!" I shouted, pumping my fist in the air.

# Chapter 9
## Getting Some Answers

Even though Tisha B'av is a fast day, girls don't have to fast before they become Bat Mitzvah at age twelve, so our bunk was still served breakfast. It was a pretty pathetic meal—just boiled eggs, bread, butter, and some limp veggies. But we couldn't complain because the waitresses were fasting and working in the hot kitchen.

I took a big gulp of milk and turned to Sarah.

"After breakfast," I said under my breath. At least

I thought it had been under my breath.

"What exactly is happening after breakfast?" Esmé said, looking at Sarah instead of at me. *Uh-oh, if I get Esmé upset at Sarah, she'll back out.*

"After breakfast, an asteroid the size of the Empire State Building is scheduled to collide with the earth," I said. "But don't worry, I made a chart, and the chances of it landing on Mah Tovu are statistically nonexistent."

"Is that another story you made up?" Jilly asked.

"Come on, leave her alone," Marley said.

Shimona frowned, giving me one of those looks that said, *This isn't helping you, Lila.*

After breakfast, we had kinos down by the lake. Kinos are special, sad Tisha B'av prayers that lament the destruction of our temples. I usually had a hard time sitting through them, but I felt like today I might connect to them more, considering what was going on with Lonny.

But I still hoped to escape early with Sarah to meet Lonny. I knew she'd work harder to save her once she met her. Besides, I missed Lonny terribly.

When we'd been there long enough, I squeezed Sarah's hand. We got up slowly, walking quietly along the path. Then I ran, hearing the crunch of sticks and dry grass under my feet and the sound of Sarah behind me. The distance to the clearing seemed shorter than it ever had been before.

Lonny stood there, grazing, as if she'd been waiting for me.

"Told you," I said.

"I believed you all along," Sarah said breathlessly, staring at my beautiful horse.

Sarah knew enough about horses to stay back as I approached Lonny. I stroked her mane.

"Good girl," I said.

I was pretty sure Lonny was happy to see me.

"I'm not going to let them hurt you," I said, wishing I felt as convinced as I sounded.

"Neither of us will," Sarah said, taking one step closer to Lonny. It felt amazing to have someone on my side besides Talia, for once.

We raced back down to the lake. The benches were overturned, as Tisha B'av is a day of mourning, and mourners are only allowed to sit low to the earth. I found an uncomfortable position and tried to concentrate on the prayers.

After a short rest in the bunk, we loaded onto the van to the senior center where we'd be listening to a Holocaust survivor tell her story. I felt bad to miss it, but Shimona told me she was recording it so I could hear it later. The van traveled an hour into town, and all anyone could talk about the whole way was the dumb canoe race.

The van dropped us off, and Sarah and I took off for the hotel down the block. We'd told the other girls we were organizing something secret. Just because everyone presumed it was color-war related didn't make it a lie.

"All of a sudden, Lila is into the camp spirit," Esmé had said sarcastically.

I didn't care. All I cared about was saving Lonny and her family.

We entered the hotel lobby, which was empty except for one table occupied by a couple and two little kids. One kid squirted a mountain of ketchup onto his plate.

"Where's your dad?" I asked Sarah.

She looked around. "Yeah, he isn't always punctual. I remember once he showed up late to my dance recital. I was so mad."

"Right," I said. Neither of my parents had ever

come late to anything I was involved with. They always said that my school shows (where I always played the part of a flower in the background that shook its petals) were their "privilege" to attend.

We sat down, far away from the table with the ketchup kid since I was wearing a white shirt. I ripped open a package of sugar, put a dab on the end of my finger, and tasted it. I was reaching for the saltshaker when a waitress came over to our table, giving us the stink eye.

"You kids sure seem young to be hanging out in a hotel on your own," she said.

I slammed the saltshaker down on the table, and it cracked.

"Oops," I said. "Sorry. I think the crack gives it character." My father had used that line the last time I'd cracked a saltshaker in a café.

The waitress put her hands on her hips. "Are you

ordering or just sitting?"

"Just sitting," Sarah said, glancing at the revolving doors of the hotel. The waitress left as a man wearing a cowboy hat approached the table.

"Sorry I'm late," he said. He pinched Sarah's cheek like she was two years old instead of ten. "Good to see you, kid."

"This is Lila," Sarah said.

He nodded. "Ted Dansky." I squinted, trying to see if I recognized him from the roundup. He didn't look particularly mean. Even with his giant hat, he was shorter than my father and skinny as a clothesline, too.

He sat next to Sarah on the plush blue bench.

"So," he said. "What was so important that we needed to meet up on Tisha B'av?"

I looked at Ted Dansky, expecting to feel anger tumbling through me, but all I saw was a man who looked parched for a drink he wasn't allowed to have. For once in my life, words failed me.

"Daddy," Sarah said, "Lila knows about the government's plans for the herd on Mah Tovu's land."

"*My* land," he said. "I own that bit of it. It's adjacent to our ranch, and that's prime grazing land, Sarah. Did you let your little friend in on that?"

I didn't like the way he called me *little*. Not one bit. I flexed my muscles.

"I-I-" Sarah's voice faltered. She cleared her throat. "Daddy, they're horses. They could die. Or be separated from their families."

"I think I know horses about as well as you do, Sarah, darling."

I reached for the saltshaker and poured some crystals into my hand. The silence felt very loud.

"I'm kind of friends with one of the horses," I

said. "Her name is Lonny. I knew she was a girl the minute we met. Sometimes you just *know* things. Like when my mother was pregnant with my little brother, and I told her I *knew* something was in her belly even though she denied it because it was too early and she was afraid it wouldn't work out?"

*Alert! Lila Grossberg's mouth is on fire! Use the fire escape!*

Ted Dansky actually smiled. There was a giant gap between his two front teeth. I tried to imagine all the things that could fit in there. Like two credit cards, a straw, and the strap of a purse.

"This is all very sweet of you, Sarah and Lila," Mr. Dansky said. "But this is our family's livelihood. I'm not looking to displace the mustangs. But if that's what I need to do to support my family, then a man's gotta do what a man's gotta do."

"Or a woman," I interrupted.

"It's just an expression," Mr. Dansky said. "In any event, we're not scheduled to move the herd until August. I suppose you girls will be finishing camp by then, right?"

We both nodded. First session at camp was over on July 30. I'd be four states away when Lonny's life changed forever.

I felt confused inside, like my large and small intestines had switched places. I didn't want Sarah's family to not have food to eat. But when I thought of Lonny, I hurt so badly.

"Can't you figure something out?" I asked. I pulled out my last piece of ammunition. "I mean, today is Tisha B'av. Us Jews have been wanderers for a long time, and we've experienced lots of persecution. You should know how that feels."

Mr. Dansky cleared his throat. "I sure do know what day it is; my throat's on fire. But you're not drawing appropriate parallels here. If there were some way I could help, I would. But I can't think of anything, barring going straight to Councilman Gold himself. He's in charge of the roundups."

He got up.

"Sarah, dear, I've got to get home to rest. I think the combo of the weather and the fasting has made me a bit dizzy around the edges."

"Okay," Sarah said. He gave her a peck on the cheek. Then he reached into his pocket and gave her a five-dollar bill.

"Get yourselves some water," he said.

"Thank you, Daddy."

Mr. Dansky smiled, then left through the same revolving doors he'd come in through.

"What was *that*?" I asked Sarah as soon as her father's hat was a blur in the distance.

"It was exactly what I told you it would be. Not

including your verbal diarrhea."

"I'm talking about the fact that you became even quieter than your regular quiet self when your dad was around."

"I'm quiet?"

I snorted. "Everyone's quiet compared to me. But you became a rabbit in front of your father."

Sarah stood up. "Let's walk to the senior home. Maybe we can still catch some of the speech."

"I don't know, Sarah. We had a deal. I feel like you barely tried."

"I tried!"

I shook my head.

"Fine," Sarah said. "So don't teach me how to read, okay? I'm hopeless, anyway."

"I'm still going to help you, and you're not hopeless. But I don't understand. You saw Lonny. I know you fell in love with that horse. Why didn't you try to help her more?"

Sarah bit her lip. "Because you don't know my father. He's not a bad man, but when he gets his mind set, there's no changing it."

"Even wild horses couldn't drag him away?" I asked, slapping my knee at my hilarious joke.

Sarah didn't laugh. "Not even wild horses."

We left the hotel and walked toward the senior center. I didn't talk, and neither did Sarah. I realized I hadn't spoken up enough for Lonny, either. It was hard to stand up to an adult, especially when I didn't understand everything. But thinking back to the moment that helicopter had threatened the herd, I knew one thing. That was so wrong.

But I'd blown the only chance I had at saving Lonny.

# Chapter 10
## Shifting Focus

What was I supposed to do now?

I had to talk to Talia, which meant telling her the truth of how I'd hurt my arm.

Talia listened as I began pouring out the whole story in the woodshop. She was sawing, and wood shavings flew toward my face.

"Put these on." She tossed me a pair of goggles. I twirled them around my good wrist and paced.

"So," I said, as I finished telling her everything,

"I was thinking that maybe you could help."

Talia unplugged her electric saw and pushed her goggles to the top of her head. She had a weird look in her eyes.

"You want my help again?" she said.

"Uh yeah. I mean, sorry, I've probably asked for too much help from you already, right? Like, if I were at the grocery store, shopping for help from Talia, my cart would be full."

"Shhh!" Talia said, raising a finger to her lips. "That's not it. I just find it odd that there was nothing in that long-winded speech of yours acknowledging that you've been hiding things from me."

I looked down at my shoes, etching patterns in the sawdust.

"Right. I'm sorry about that."

"What you did was dangerous. But you know what's just as dangerous?"

"What?"

"Lying to someone you trust. Lying to someone who trusts you."

Something welled up in my throat, and I swallowed, hard.

"It's . . . just something I do. I lie without even knowing I'm doing it, if that makes any sense. It's even the first syllable of my name!"

Talia pulled me down to sit next to her on the wooden bench.

"Well," she said. "Maybe it's time to change your name, then. And I don't mean that literally."

I nodded. "Does—does that mean you won't help me?"

She rested a hand on my shoulder.

"No. I want to help. I care about those horses, and I care about you. I'm just not sure of what I can do. To be honest, Risa and the other honchos over here aren't going to get themselves all stitched up over wild horses."

My shoulders slumped. She was right. Risa's husband was a rancher, too.

The fan clicked and whirred as Talia and I sat, thinking.

"Wait a second," Talia said. "You know what I think?"

"If I knew what you thought, I'd be living in your brain, and that would be weird."

"Also, it's crowded enough in there, trust me," she said.

I half smiled and waited for Talia's idea.

"You said Ted Dansky mentioned that Councilman Gold was the only one who might be able to help, right?"

"Yeah, but why would some councilman ever listen to *me*? And how would I even—"

"Just a second," Talia said. "There's a girl in your bunk—Esmé—I happen to have overheard that her father is a councilman. What's her last n—"

I jumped up. "Gold! Esmé Gold!"

Talia jumped up, too. "This is perfect!"

I couldn't believe it. The person in charge of this whole program was Esmé's father? I would—I could—I sat back down, exhaling slowly.

"This is actually bad news. Esmé's not the type to want to help anyone, especially me. And she doesn't even believe that Lonny is real."

Talia picked a wooden airplane missing a wing off of the table, turning it in her hands.

"Well, I can help with that," Talia said. "I can tell her—"

I held up my hand. "No way. No adults necessary. I mean, thanks, anyway."

Talia nodded, setting the airplane back down.

"Yeah, I get it. Well, you think about it. Maybe you'll change your mind about speaking to Esmé. In the meantime—I think you need to throw yourself into camp, Lila. Color war will be breaking out any minute. The summer's almost over. You may not be able to save these horses, but at least you can salvage the rest of your camp experience."

Talia was beginning to sound like all the other adults I knew. She loved horses, although she didn't love Lonny a quarter as much as I did. But she knew she didn't stand a chance against the ranchers. According to her, they simply had too much power in this neck of woods.

I nodded slowly. "Okay. I'll try. But can you promise to visit Lonny for me?"

She set down what she was working on and took her goggles off.

"Every day."

I hopped back to the bunk, alternating feet, taking care not to fall. I couldn't believe Councilman Gold was Esmé's father! Not that it changed anything. If only it weren't Esmé ...

The girls' campus was decorated with blue-and-white streamers, as everyone was waiting for the color war breakout. Last year, an airplane had flown over camp, dropping leaflets with all the team information on them. The year before that, two local policemen had pretended to arrest Talia for using too much local lumber in her woodshop for color-war breakout. I wondered what it would be this year. I took a deep breath before stepping back into the bunk.

*Focus on camp.*

"So, uh, what's with the canoe race?" I said loudly as the screen door slammed behind me.

"Really?" Ariella asked. "What do you mean?"

"I mean, I'd like to be involved in the canoe race. You know, whichever team our bunk is on." I pointed to my bum wrist. "Obviously I can't paddle."

Esmé was lying on her bed, wearing the fanciest headphones I'd ever seen. She sat up and took them off.

"Seriously, Lila? You're waking up now? We've been training for nearly three weeks!"

"I was busy!" I said. "Taking care of my horse."

"Right," Jilly said. "Your horse."

Even Marley shook her head at me.

I looked at Sarah, knowing that there was no way she'd admit the truth in front of everyone, but still hoping. I'd been practicing reading with her these past few days, and I thought I was a mighty good teacher, if I did say so myself.

Sarah gave a slight shake of her head, letting me know she'd be no help. Admitting she was my friend would be like choosing to step in dog poop and walking around with it stuck to the bottom of her sneaker.

I sat on my bed and gave my lucky toucan a squeeze. Suddenly the PA system crackled: "Everyone get outside and catch the balloons. It's color war!"

We raced outside. There was a truck at the edge of the girls' campus, blowing thousands or maybe millions of blue-and-white balloons all over. Kids ran, frantically grabbing balloons and popping them, so the campus sounded like it was in the middle of a world war. I ran, snatching balloons and jumping on them to pop them. The team lists were folded up inside. Our bunk was on the blue team. I quickly checked the staff list. Talia was on the white team. I looked around at all the happy kids. I guess I looked happy, too, from the outside, but inside I felt like a popped balloon. How could I concentrate on color war when nobody liked me and when Lonny was in danger? This summer at Mah Tovu hadn't turned out to be as bad as Camp Reyut. It was worse.

I went to call my parents, but neither answered their phone.

"Don't forget to put on your blue shirts," Shimona said when I got back to the bunk.

"I'm not feeling so well," I said, crawling into bed.

I didn't need a blue shirt. I was blue all over.

There was no way to fix this summer.

*Maybe you can figure it out, God.*

Maybe He would send me a sign. But I couldn't even imagine how He could help.

# Chapter 11
## Punch It in the Nose

The cheering at breakfast the next morning was so loud, the *food* was scared.

"You still under the weather?" Shimona asked me. I'd already missed the color-war cheer activity last night.

"Yeah."

"You should go to the nurse," Marley said.

I shrugged. There was no cure for my particular sickness.

I ran back to the bunk to clean up, as I'd promised Sarah I'd study with her afterward. When I entered the bunkhouse, Esmé was sitting on her bed, touching the picture of the horse hanging above it. She looked sad. For a second, I considered spilling what I knew about her father and asking her to help, but then I remembered who she was. Anyway, everyone barged into the bunk, and Esmé snapped out of it. I tried to straighten up my stuff, since cleanup points were doubled during color war. Everyone left to practice for the canoe race. Sarah made some excuse, and we stayed behind to study reading. The girls' campus was like a ghost town.

"Wow," I said. "You're devoted."

Sarah flipped her hair. "I already know how to canoe. I don't really need to practice. But you've been the best reading teacher I've ever had. I've learned more from you in a week than I did from all the tutors I've worked with. You make it fun."

Well, yeah. I did act out all the letters, and I made up a bunch of nonsense words that had Sarah giggling her face off.

"Thanks."

There was a knock on the door of the bunk. Sarah threw her book under the bed, and we sprang apart like opposite-pole magnets. It was Jeannie, the lady who delivered the mail.

"Packages," she said, leaving a stack by the door. I raced to check them out.

The top package was for Esmé, all wrapped in glittery purple paper. The one underneath it had my name written on it with my mother's messy curlicues.

I tore at the box, pulling out a giant bag of Shugabirds, a box of granola bars, and a purple envelope. I ripped the envelope open and pulled out a piece of Mario stationery.

Dear Lila,
If at first you don't succeed, punch it in the nose.
Love, Mom, Dad, and Adam

Dad had doodled a man getting boxed in the face under his message, and it made me crack up.

"Thank you, God!" I cried. I knew my parents weren't referring to saving Lonny, since I hadn't shared that with them yet, but messages from God were open to interpretation, in my opinion.

Sarah took her books back out. "I really have to get down to the lake soon or Esmé will start getting suspicious."

Esmé. Sarah.

Of course. The answer was staring me in the face. Why hadn't I thought of her right away?

"Sarah!" I said, tugging at her arm. "I have an idea about helping Lonny! Remember when your father said only Councilman Gold could possibly help us?"

Sarah didn't look enthusiastic.

"Yeah?"

"Well, did you realize Councilman Gold shares a last name with Esmé? And a lot of DNA."

Sarah grabbed my lucky toucan off my bed and slammed it against the wall, killing a mosquito.

"Hey!" I shouted, grabbing my toucan. "That's not a flyswatter!"

"Sorry."

She sat on my bed. "Listen, Lila, I see where you're going with this. Of course, I know Esmé's father is Councilman Gold; I've been friends with her since we were in diapers. Although, honestly, I had no idea he was involved with the mustangs. Esmé's parents treat her like royalty. So yeah, she *could* do something. But in case you haven't noticed,

Esmé's not exactly the helpful sort. Not to mention, she's not your biggest fan."

I thought back to the moment I'd caught Esmé staring at that picture of a horse. I remembered how eager she was to come see Lonny, even though she didn't really believe me.

"What if Esmé doesn't want to help another person, but she'd be willing to help a horse?" I asked.

Sarah shook her head. "I doubt it. Besides, she doesn't even believe you about the horses, and there's no way you're getting her to the forest again."

I looked at Sarah.

"She would listen to you. I know it."

Sarah frowned. "I'm not telling Esmé I'm in cahoots with you. I'm not that brave."

My heart started sinking. I could feel it sliding down, into my stomach, then down into my right leg. I pictured Lonny's face, her shiny coat. My head filled with the clatter of helicopter blades. The answer felt so close and so far, all at the same time.

*Think, Lila.*

"Earth to Lila," Sarah said. "They need me to practice for the race, so can we learn already?"

The canoe race.

"Hello?" Sarah said, waving her hand in front of my face. "Anyone in there? Besides Lonny?"

*Yes! That's it!*

I felt my heart climbing out of my leg. It reached my stomach, which was better than nothing.

I bounced onto the bed, feeling it springy underneath me. I ripped open a bag of Shugabirds.

I had an idea. It was farfetched. It might fail. But I wasn't going to let Lonny's life get ruined without trying to punch that helicopter in the nose.

# Chapter 12
## The Great Canoe Race

Everything at breakfast the next day was blue or white, depending on which team had prepared it. The milk was blue, and the blueberries were covered in powdered sugar. The cereal was tan, but the white team was passing it off as white. The hard-boiled eggs were blue. In short, breakfast was gross.

"I'm too nervous to eat," Esmé said, pushing away her cereal swimming in blue milk.

"I just want this race to be over," Becky said.

"Come on," Marley said. "It will be fun!"

"If we win," Esmé said.

We cleaned up, and everyone raced back to the bunk. Today, I wasn't the only one in a hurry.

I figured I'd better get off to a good start with my bunkmates, so I worked hard to clean up my space. I even swept under my bed and spritzed the air with freshener fifteen times.

"Are you coming to watch the race?" Jilly asked as she tugged the air freshener away from me.

"In a sense," I said.

Esmé pulled a tiara out of her hair-thingy box. "How do you watch a race 'in a sense'?" She fixed the tiara to her hair and looked in the mirror.

I was itching to go. I pulled my blanket so tight, you could bounce a basketball on it.

"I'm wearing this crown because we're going to be winners today," Esmé said. "Gather, guys!"

The girls gathered in the middle of the bunk and made a pile of their hands, then shouted "Blue team!" as they pulled them away. Everyone except me, of course.

The PA system crackled again.

"Bunks 4A, 4B, 5A, 5B, 6A, 6B, 6C, and all bunk sevens, please head down to the waterfront for the great canoe race!"

We headed out the door. I followed, as if I were going with them, but when we got to the dirt road, I squeezed Sarah's hand then turned left instead of right. The good thing about not having friends? I was invisible. Nobody noticed me leaving.

I raced to the woodshop. I wasn't making the mistake of lying to Talia again. Last night, I shared my plan with her, and she agreed to help me. I banged on the door, but nobody answered. The door was open, so I walked inside, but everything was quiet: the tools locked away in their cabinets, the tables clear. She said she would be here!

Near the phone hanging on the wall was a pen and paper. I jotted a quick note.

I came at the arranged time, but you weren't here.
I'm sorry. I have to do this. Meet me if you can. Lila.

I dashed out of the woodshop, my heart thudding in my chest. Well, at least my heart had finally returned to its usual location. When I reached the woods, I ran.

"Lonny!" I called at the clearing, hoping she'd be there, but she wasn't. I didn't have much time. The halter and saddle were hanging on the tree, and there was no way I'd be able to carry them through the woods to Lonny. I began the trek, following faded hoofprints and my memory of the walk we'd taken together. I was so busy concentrating, I almost knocked into her.

"Lonny!"

I wrapped my arms around her neck, breathing in her horse smell.

"You need to come with me," I said. "This is my only chance of helping you. Understand?"

Lonny looked at me. Then she nodded. No joke. Okay, maybe she was shaking off a parasite, but that's what it felt like. We walked together, back through the woods until we reached the clearing.

"There isn't enough time for me to walk with you," I told her. "I need to ride you."

I took the halter and saddle off the hook and lugged them over.

"Let me do this," I said, gently but firmly. "This is how I can save *you*."

She bent her head. I stood on the stump and put the halter on her, then lifted the saddle, laying it on her back as softly as I could. She didn't budge.

"Good girl, Lonny."

I fastened it around her belly just like I'd seen Talia do. Then I waited. Ten minutes passed, then fifteen, then twenty. I wanted to hop, jump, and run, but I needed to give her time, getting to know the feel of something on her back.

"Now," I said. "I'm going to mount, okay?"

I held out a Shugabird in my palm and felt Lonny's rough tongue as she slurped it up. I fed her a cube of sugar I'd swiped at breakfast, too. Then, I put my foot in the stirrup and grabbed the horn of the saddle. My heart was beating as fast as a fire engine on the way to a five-alarm fire.

I hoisted myself fast. Up and over! That's what the lady in the video had said. I slid my feet into the stirrups. Everything felt different up here, sitting on top of this living, breathing animal. Like, before, I'd been this tiny ant crawling through the grass, and now I was hanging from the trees, and I could see the universe from one end to the other.

"Giddyap!" I shouted, gently tapping Lonny with my heels.

She didn't move.

"Go!" I shouted, digging my heels in more firmly, tugging the reins in the direction I needed her to move.

She snorted and lolled her head from side to side. She took one small step forward, then another.

"Good!" I called, more forcefully, my feet slapping against her flank. She began to trot through the woods, back the same way I'd come. I bounced up and down as the trees rose on both sides of us and Lonny picked her way through the rocky forest. Finally, we reached the edge of the woods. I pulled the reins left, and she turned down the dirt road that led to the lake. It was eerily quiet. Everyone in camp was either at the lake or off doing some other color-war activity. We got closer to the lake, and the noise grew. I could see campers from afar, tiny specks of blue and white. It was now or never.

"Giddyap!" I shouted. I leaned forward.

And Lonny went. She cantered, and I held on for dear life, my heart galloping right along with her until it settled into a steady rhythm. The wind felt like a thousand fans blowing on me, and the trees looked like giant stalks of broccoli. I held tight to Lonny, feeling a smile cracking my face in two as we broke through the trees and she whinnied louder than Risa's megaphone. We got within shouting distance of the crowd.

"Whoa!" I cried, tugging the reins. Lonny stopped. This humongous animal was listening to little old Lila Grossberg. *Nobody* listened to me! I felt like I'd been handed a giant ice cream cone, loaded to the clouds with Shugabirds.

The crowd turned around in waves, everyone staring at me sitting on top of a gorgeous mare.

Kids were murmuring, and nobody was even looking at the lake anymore. They were saying things like, "What?" and "Where?" and "Why?" It was the weirdest thing that, for once, everyone else had all the questions, and I had all the answers.

Risa pushed her way through the crowd and approached with her megaphone.

"What is the meaning of this?" she asked, talking into the megaphone even though she was about six feet away from us.

"Uh, this is Lonny?" I said, scanning the crowd. I couldn't tell the story until I saw Esmé.

Risa took out her rule book, flipping through.

"Rule number two sixty-four is not bringing zoo animals onto campgrounds," she said, "but I'm sure there's also something here about riding horses unsupervised. Except we never had horses, so it might not be in the book yet. We will have to make immediate revisions."

I spotted my bunk coming into shore, their canoes spray-painted blue. People turned their attention back to the race.

"Bunk 5B, third place!" the team captain shouted on her megaphone. So they hadn't won. Third place wasn't bad, but I knew it wasn't enough for them.

Esmé dragged hers and Sarah's canoe onto land and set down her oars. Then she took off her tiara, turned around, and tossed it into the lake. Such a drama queen! Sarah took off her life jacket. Esmé lifted her head and saw me sitting on Lonny's back. There should have been mood music playing in the background. Instead, I just flashed her a goofy grin. Lonny snorted and pinned her ears. The crowd was making her nervous. If she got wild, nobody would want to help her, and it wouldn't even be her fault.

"Excuse me," Esmé said, pushing her way through the crowd. "Excuse me."

Risa was still figuring out which ticket to write me when Esmé approached.

"So you were telling the truth," she said, looking at Lonny, not at me.

"Yes," I said. "Also no."

She looked up at me now. "As usual, you're not making sense."

I felt Lonny, standing peacefully beneath me, and it made me calm. It made Esmé's words not matter.

"I lied about being an equestrian," I said. "But you already know that. I told the truth about finding wild horses here. And I guess now I'm some kind of equestrian. By the way—the word was *gallop*."

Esmé gave a small smile. "Can I touch her?"

I wasn't sure how Lonny would feel about that, but I reminded myself why I was doing all this to begin with.

"Yeah, just be careful."

Esmé frowned. "I know how to handle horses." She approached Lonny from the side and leaned her head gently against her, closing her eyes.

"I-I had a horse like this once," she said. "Her name was Sugar. My dad adopted her for me. She also used to be a mustang. But she—"

Esmé opened her eyes, and they were filled with tears.

"She got hurt, and we had to put her down."

"Wow," I said. "I'm really sorry."

She wiped her eyes with the back of her hand. "Yeah, well, my father could just buy me another one. But no horse could ever replace Sugar. So whatever."

By now, my whole bunk was standing around me, Lonny, and Esmé. Everyone else was busy congratulating the winners of the race. Honestly, I'd thought out getting Lonny to the lake, but I hadn't planned exactly what I'd say. My brain's the sort that can only handle one scene of the movie at a time.

But I had to speak before Risa blared into her megaphone and Lonny bolted.

"I get it," I said to Esmé. "Lonny's life is in danger, too." I petted her mane.

"What?" she said. "Why?"

Suddenly, Sarah stepped forward. She took a deep breath. "Because the government is clearing the land of horses so the ranchers can rent it for their cattle."

Esmé spun around to look at Sarah. "What? How do you know about this? Wait. Have you been hanging out with Lila and her horse?"

Sarah's voice shook as she answered. "Yeah. Lila's actually really nice, interesting, and fun. And, Esmé, we need your father's help to protect Lonny and her herd."

"What?" Esmé said. "What does my father have to do with any of this?"

"He's the one in charge of relocating the horses," I said.

Esmé shook her head. "Impossible. My father loves horses. He would never do anything to hurt them."

Sarah took Esmé's hand.

"It's true," she said. "I'm sorry, Esmé."

The megaphone crackled.

"I can't find any specific offense you have violated," Risa said. "Horses are not zoo animals."

Lonny, startled, bucked. I held on tight.

"But I will immediately amend the rule book,"

Risa said. "So this won't happen again."

People streamed up from the lake, and the little kids began approaching Lonny. I looked at Sarah and Esmé. Esmé seemed so confused. Despite everything, my heart hurt for her.

"Esmé, Sarah, I need your help," I said. This was it. The moment it would all either fall apart or come together. "There's something I need to show you. Follow me, but keep a distance."

I turned Lonny around, and we trotted back up the road. I whispered a short prayer, then peeked behind me. Esmé and Sarah were right there. Risa was too busy scribbling in her rule book to notice us leaving. I turned right at my favorite tree. We rounded the bend into Lonny's favorite clearing.

"Keep going," I said to Lonny. Into the woods. Down the path. Out into the marsh.

"Whoa," I said. Lonny stopped. I dismounted.

"Esmé, can you help me out with this?" I asked. She nodded, and together we removed Lonny's halter and saddle. Our eyes met, and I could see the hurt in them—for Sugar, for her father's involvement in all of this, and, hopefully, for Lonny.

"Now go," I said to Lonny, kissing her on the side of her nose. She just stared at me.

"Come on," I said. "Go home!"

She whinnied, then broke through the tall brush and disappeared. My heart ached, as I didn't know if I'd ever ride her again.

"Where are the rest of them?" Esmé asked. She knew Lonny wouldn't be alone.

I held my finger to my lips and tiptoed to the edge of the marsh, followed by Esmé and Sarah. I pushed the brush aside. Lonny had rejoined her herd. They were racing back and forth, kicking up dirt under their hooves. Their bodies shone in the afternoon sun. It was like watching gold ripple across the earth.

"Oh," Esmé said. "I've never seen anything so beautiful in my entire life."

"Yeah," I said, though my eyes were only on Lonny. She looked happy. Free.

"The ranchers want them out," I said. "The herd will be separated. Not all will survive. Those that do will be put into holding pens, and they'll never run free again. It's happening in August."

Esmé shook her head. "It doesn't make sense. My father's a good man."

Sarah rested a hand on Esmé's shoulder. "My father loves horses, too. But the wild horses compete for their cattle's grazing land. It's all just really complicated."

Esmé looked at me. "Yeah," she said. "I guess life really is complicated sometimes."

"Trust me, I know about that," I said, thinking

about Herman and my "Extra-Creative Fun Brain."

"I can't believe that in a few days these horses won't be running free anymore," Sarah said.

It was the perfect opening line. Sarah had thrown the pitch. Now I needed to hit it out of the park. "Unless," I said, looking at Esmé, "someone puts a stop to it."

Esmé's mouth hung open as she watched the horses play. I was sure she was thinking of Sugar.

"We need to do something big," she said breathlessly. She pulled her eyes from the horses. "Sugar was injured in a wild-horses roundup. We tried to rehabilitate her, but it was too late. She'd been run too many hours over rough terrain and—" She pulled herself up till she was standing super straight. "I'm going to speak to my father."

This was the moment I'd been waiting for. Esmé and I were on the same page, and I was ready to reveal the next stage of my plan.

"What if we open up the grand color-war finale to the public?" I said. "And we tell them about the plight of the wild horses."

Esmé jumped up and down. "Yeah!" she said, looking back at the horses. "And I have an even better idea of how to get the message across."

Of *course* Esmé had a better idea.

If it could help Lonny and her family, though, I didn't care if the idea came from Risa and she blared it out of her megaphone. Okay, maybe not her, but anyone else.

# Chapter 13
## Operation Save the Mustangs

It's not like I was a different person. I still fidgeted, and things still slid out of my mouth like otters on a cliff. But things had changed. Sarah was officially my friend now, even though Esmé was giving her a bit of a cold shoulder over keeping the horses and our friendship a secret from her. We were super busy with Operation Save the Mustangs, but Sarah and I still made time to practice reading. She was working so hard. Once the other girls in the bunk realized I was telling the truth about the horses, they started warming to me, too. I kind of felt like I was working hard to save Lonny's life, and meanwhile, she was busy helping me with mine.

It was drizzly the day of color-war cantata—when both teams presented their team song, banner, and dramatic production. But my mood was anything but damp. I raced to the woodshop after morning prayers. Talia was sanding a wooden box. She shook her head when she saw me.

"You're lucky I like you so much," she said.

Talia couldn't believe that I had ridden Lonny on my own, but she also couldn't be *too* angry since she'd stood me up. The crazy thing was, she didn't even have some amazing excuse, like she'd woken up with her eye swollen shut, or she'd found a snake inside her pillowcase. She'd just overslept. Even adults goof up!

I put my hands on my hips. "My parents say they can't help but love me."

Talia turned off the sander and set the box down.

"You *are* lovable. You also remind me a lot of myself at your age." She pushed a stray red curl out of her eyes. "I was *just like you.* I said all the wrong things at all the wrong times, and my brain was always a few steps ahead of itself or behind itself. They didn't have names for these things when I was a kid, but I think you might know what I mean?"

Of *course* I knew what she meant. But I couldn't believe it. Everyone loved Talia. Even though the girls were coming around, it was like I was a fungus growing on their feet they were agreeing to tolerate.

"Some people still find me to be a bit much," she said. "But I don't pay them any attention. Enough people appreciate my uniqueness. I look in their direction, and all's good."

I tried to imagine my brain hopping around in an adult body.

"Trust me," Talia said. "It's just going to be up and up for you from here on out."

That made me feel as happy as a mustang running through a zillion empty acres.

"Now let's go see if we can find Lonny," Talia said. "It's our last chance."

Talia had helped a ton for our big day today. She'd convinced Risa to open things up to the public, telling her it was good publicity for the camp. And she was still willing to accompany me to the forest, since I was under threat of expulsion from camp if I went out there alone. Yesterday, Talia had taken me to the marsh to watch Lonny from afar. I was grateful to Talia for a thousand things.

Lonny was in the clearing, as if she'd been waiting for me all along. I approached her and wrapped my arms around her neck. Yesterday, Talia had helped me drag the saddle back here, so we had Lonny saddled up within moments today. Talia wouldn't let me ride her out of the clearing, so we just walked in circles, my heart beating to the rhythm of her trot.

"We'd better go," Talia said, tapping her watch.

I dismounted, and we removed Lonny's saddle. I didn't want to leave her. I had no idea when, or even if, I would see her again. Camp was ending in three days, and if we didn't change things . . .

"Get out of your brain, Lila," Talia said. "We have things to do."

I hugged Lonny goodbye. Talia was right.

Back in the bunk, Jilly gave me a stink eye.

"Where'd you disappear to?" she asked. She was pouring glitter on a poster board that read WILD ABOUT MUSTANGS!

I could have kicked myself. My bunkmates were working to help me, and I'd run off again. A lie slid around on my tongue. Things like *I got bitten by a tarantula* trotted around my brain, but I looked at everyone hard at work, and I imagined myself calm and steady on Lonny's silky back.

"I went to say goodbye to Lonny. I'm sorry for leaving you guys. I'll work double time now."

Jilly nodded, and I dug in.

Two hours later, we were setting things up on the softball field. Each bunk was entitled to one presentation to gather points for their team for cantata—the final event of color war. Talia was setting up a giant screen, which nearly toppled over on her head. I hung signs as Marley and Becky helped Talia. Esmé was pacing, waiting for her father to arrive. Everyone was stoked that he was coming, even Risa, who wore red lipstick for the occasion.

Marley helped me connect the lights to turn on our MARVELOUS MUSTANGS! sign. I was glad for the gray afternoon since the flashing lights wouldn't have shown up in bright light.

Marley and Ariella raced toward the softball field, holding clipboards.

"We got five hundred signatures for the online Save the Mustangs petition I started!" Ariella cried, and we all applauded.

We finished setting up our booth and waited for Councilman Gold to arrive. Esmé said her father was willing to help. He even had a plan, but it was up to us and our event to get him the support he needed from the ranchers and the other officials.

I sat on third base, chewing on a hangnail when I felt someone nudge my shoulder. I looked up.

"Hey," Esmé said, squinting down at me.

"Hey back."

"You okay?"

"Nah. I've got Lonny on the brain."

"I get it."

Esmé was wearing a ridiculous pink feather boa around her neck.

"You look like you're going to the opera," I said. "I mean, oops, sorry."

Esmé shrugged. "It's fine. I know it's ugly. But my father bought it for me. It'll make him happy to see me wearing it. I'm still upset at him for all this. But I guess people do what they have to do. At least he's trying to fix things."

"Right," I said.

"Anyway. I just wanted to say thanks for, you know, doing all this for the horses. Well, my dad could come any minute, so we should man our stations." She kicked the dirt with the toe of her silver-studded sneakers and walked away.

It was interesting that some people wore their hearts on their sleeves while others kept them buried under layers of feathers and rhinestones—but they were good ones, too.

"He's coming!" Jilly shouted.

I raced to the dugout and picked up the megaphone. When we'd asked Risa to borrow it, she'd reacted like we'd asked if we could saw off her arm. But she'd parted with it for the sake of Councilman Gold.

A group of about ten men and women, all wearing cowboy and cowgirl hats, were coming our way. In the center was a tall, bearded man, his belly hanging over a brass buckled belt, wearing high boots. When he saw Esmé, he held out his arms like he expected her to come running, but he dropped them when she held back.

"Hello, princess," he said. "Love that boa!"

"Thank you for coming, Daddy. I appreciate you trying to help the herd."

They sounded so formal; they should have been wearing tuxedos.

I turned on the megaphone.

*Give me courage, God. K? Thanks!*

"Welcome to the blue team's Save the Mustangs Campaign! We know that livestock and horses are competing for the same grazing land here in North Carolina, and we're aware of the roundups that are taking place. But we're here to talk about one specific herd—a beautiful family of horses living by the marsh just north of Camp Mah Tovu. They may not have the best grazing facilities, but they're happy, and most of all, they're free!"

I passed the megaphone to Ariella.

"The American mustang is a symbol of our country!" she cried. "They fought in our wars! They helped us till our fields!"

Talia and I had written this speech. I could see the officials nodding along.

"The picture is far more complicated than just saying resources are scarce," Ariella continued. Jilly started handing out the flyers we'd typed up with all the myths people believed about wild mustangs. I watched as the officials scanned the pages.

"We know we can't fix all the problems in the world. But we're asking you to help us start, one herd at a time. This is our herd."

Talia pressed play on the computer. The screen filled with a beautiful video of Lonny racing under a setting sun, the sky purple above her. I heard a gasp from the crowd. I looked at Esmé. The PowerPoint presentation had been her idea. Photos and videos of our beautiful horses filled the screen. They ran in time with the music, their manes flopping, their legs looking like they weren't even touching the ground.

"They're glorious!" someone in the group shouted, and everyone applauded.

When the presentation was over, we showed them the petitions, and Talia fielded the more complicated questions for us.

I knew there was no simple solution for the mustangs, but I had to hope something could change.

A familiar man emerged from the crowd.

"I hear you've got a magic way with words," Mr. Danksky said to me. "My wife and I can't thank you enough for helping Sarah."

"I don't know about magic," I said. "I mean, I'm not like an enchanted fairy godmother or anything. But I'm a good teach—"

Sarah clamped a hand over my mouth. "She means to say thanks."

"Fancy meeting you here, Dansky," Councilman Gold said, dropping a thick hand on his shoulder. "What do you think of this predicament our dear daughters have brought to light?"

Sarah and I exchanged glances.

"We'd all like a solution that suits everyone," Mr. Dansky said. "Even us ranchers."

Sarah flung her arms around her father's neck.

"Thank you, Daddy!"

He looked awkward, like he was being attacked by an octopus. But he also looked happy.

"Well, meet us at town hall at eight this evening," Councilman Gold said.

"I'll be there," said Mr. Dansky.

Then Risa appeared, grabbing the megaphone.

"Our esteemed guests are invited to the dining room for a feast of fish and chips," she said. I'm pretty sure she also gave her megaphone a kiss.

"We'll pass," Councilman Gold said, as Esmé made a gagging motion at her father, instructing him not to take Risa up on her offer. He looked at the crowd of people he'd come with. "We have important business to take care of. So much to do, so little time. Esmé, my love, I'll keep you posted."

She took two steps toward her father, and I could tell that she was trying to forgive him. I thought she might hug him, but instead she reached out her hand for a shake. He took it between both of his own and squeezed.

"Pleasure doing business with you, ma'am." Then he lowered his voice to a whisper, but I still heard him say, "I'm mighty proud of you, Esmé."

I watched them all walk away, their boots digging holes in the grass.

I didn't know what would happen with Lonny and her herd. But I knew I'd done everything I could.

# Chapter 14
## Canoe Practice

The water on the lake sparkled when you watched it from a distance, but up close in a canoe, it looked like a green swamp.

"There could be things hiding in here," I said as I hung my oar in the water. "Like the Loch Ness monster. Do you see that huge bump in the water?" I screeched and stood up.

"Lila dropped her oar," Shimona shouted from a nearby canoe.

Esmé and Becky sat in a nearby canoe that floated lazily.

"It's a patch of algae," Becky said. "Seriously, Lila."

I squinted at the blob. It *was* just a patch of algae. It definitely wasn't a monster. I closed my eyes, grossed out by what I was about to do. But I wasn't going to make anyone rescue me this time. Not when things were finally turning around for me. My wrist was healed, and I wasn't wearing my Ace bandage, so there was nothing stopping me. I jumped over the side of the canoe into the water.

"Li-la, Li-la, Li-la," my bunkmates began chanting all around me. I bobbed in the water, the sun reflecting off of my orange life jacket. I grabbed the oar and held it up in the air victoriously before depositing it in the canoe. Sarah held out her hand and pulled hard until I tumbled in, panting.

"Did I tell you guys I lied about knowing how to canoe?" I said.

"Well, you have a whole year to practice," Marley called out from the canoe she shared with Shimona. "Are there any lakes in New Jersey?"

"Seriously?" Esmé said, as she expertly turned her canoe around.

Esmé wasn't the sort to mince words. But I noticed that instead of getting insulted, Marley laughed. At herself. Or maybe with herself. I wondered if that was something I could learn to do.

I watched Sarah's oars cutting circles in the water, and I tried to copy her. I concentrated, attempting to ignore the woods on our left, where Lonny was hopefully grazing happily. Sarah's oars made little ripples in the water that fanned out into bigger and bigger ripples. It made me think of how one small movement could sometimes grow into something humongous. Like telling a lie. Or looking into a beautiful horse's brown eyes.

"I think you're getting the hang of it, Lila," Jilly called, smiling.

"Third place," Esmé muttered. "No way will I stand for third place next year."

I wondered if I would be back here next near. I wondered if Lonny would be here next year, too. I couldn't consider any other possibility.

We strained to hear the announcement from campus: *"Phone call for Esmé Gold in the main office."*

We all looked at one another. The camp usually only paged counselors for phone calls. If they were calling Esmé, it was important.

"Well?" Sarah said. "What are we waiting for? Let's go get that phone call."

"Turn!" Sarah called to me. I whispered a silent prayer as we rushed our boats around.

# Chapter 15
## Goodbye, Lonny

Talia stood back, giving me my space as I leaned against Lonny's flank.

"So," I said to her. "I have some good news and some bad news. Which do you want first? The good news? Okay. We did it! You're not going to be helicopter-raced out of here! I mean, you *are* going to be removed from this area. But that's not bad news. You'll be moved, gently, to a marsh not too far from here, where you and your herd can live out your lives in freedom. There's more grazing land there. And your herd will be protected forever. Councilman Gold and the ranchers came to a special agreement to fix the problem. As if anyone could ever call *you* a problem."

She nuzzled her head into my neck.

"And now for the bad news," I said. I blinked hard. I'd promised myself I wouldn't cry. "I don't know if or when I'll see you again. I mean, I'll be back at Mah Tovu next year. My friends say I'd better come back. But you'll be somewhere else."

I touched her nose. "I'll look for you. But if I don't find you, I'll know in my heart that you're okay."

Then I wrapped my arms around her neck and held her tight, my heart feeling full and empty.

"I'll miss you," I said.

She snorted, which I took to mean she would miss me, too.

Talia and I walked back to camp in silence. Before we reached the campgrounds, she gave me a giant hug.

"You're a superstar," she said.

"I have good role models."

My bunkmates were excited, even though we were loading our suitcases onto the buses. Everyone was so happy we'd saved the mustangs, it made us forget about the pain of leaving new friends behind—like a sunburst during a storm.

"You're still tutoring me remotely, right?" Sarah said before I got on the bus.

"Every day. You're my best and only student."

"And friend!" Sarah said.

"That too! Sometimes when you have a lot of words to say, only some of them come out, and—"

"Got it!" Sarah shouted, laughing and punching me in the arm.

We got on the bus, cheering and singing as the engine started. Risa shouted into her megaphone, but nobody heard what she was saying. Jilly and Marley passed me their autograph books, and I passed them mine. I imagined my parents waiting for me in the airport. I couldn't wait to finally tell them *everything*. The bus began pulling away, and I saw Esmé, waving.

I waved back.

I closed my eyes, imagining myself on Lonny's back, flying, floating away from Camp Mah Tovu. "Thank you, Lonny," I whispered to the wind. "You have no idea what you've done for me." Maybe there weren't any supernatural horses in Mah Tovu, but I could have sworn I heard Lonny whispering on the wind right back at me, "*I feel exactly the same way*," as the bus bumped down the road, taking me home.